Postman Pat's Messy Day

Story by *John Cunliffe*
Pictures by *Joan Hickson*

From the original Television designs by **Ivor Wood**

André Deutsch/Hippo Books

Published simultaneously in hardback by André
Deutsch Limited, 105-106 Great Russell Street, London
WC1B 3LJ and in paperback by Hippo Books, Scholastic
Publications Limited, 10 Earlham Street, London WC2H 9RX
in 1986

Reprinted 1987

Text copyright © 1986 John Cunliffe
Illustrations copyright © 1986 by André Deutsch Limited,
Scholastic Publications Limited and Woodland Animations
Limited

ISBN 0 233 97992 1 (hardback)
ISBN 0 590 70589 X (paperback)

Made and printed in Belgium by Proost
Typeset in Souvenir by Keyline Graphics

It was a nice day.

The sun was coming out.

"Lovely," said Pat.

He put his sun-glasses on.

Pat was on his way, in his red van.

He had a big bag of letters and parcels.

Everyone looked out for Pat, and said,

"I hope he has something for me,

today."

Jess liked the sun, too.

He sat in his basket, next to Pat.

The sun shone on Jess.

It made him warm.

It made him purr.

Jess washed his paws.

He washed his ears.

He twitched his whiskers.

Pat stopped at Ted's house.

There were two letters and a parcel for Ted.

Pat knocked at Ted's door.

There was no answer.

"Hello!" called Pat. "Anyone at home?"

Pat opened the door.

"Hello, Ted, are you there?"

Ted was not there.

"That's funny," said Pat.

"He must be about, somewhere."

He put the letters and the parcel

on the table.

"We'll have to find him," said Pat.
"He has to sign for that parcel."
Pat and Jess went to look for Ted in the
garden.
They saw a magpie, a snail, and a
squirrel, but no Ted.

Pat and Jess went to look for Ted in his
garage.

They looked in Ted's car.

They looked under Ted's car.

Jess saw a mouse run to its hole,

but he could not catch it.

Pat saw Ted's tool-kit, open on the

bench.

But they did not see Ted.

"I know," said Pat, "he might be round
the back, sunbathing on the lawn."
Pat and Jess went round to the back.
There was a ladder at the side of the
house.
There was a deck chair on the lawn.
There was an empty glass,
and a book, next to it.
But there was no Ted.

"Where can he be?" said Pat.

"Hello!" said Ted.

Pat jumped. Jess put his claws out.

"Has that parcel come?" said Ted.

Where was he? Pat looked up and down, but he could not see Ted. His voice was near.

"I'm up here," said Ted.

Pat looked up. Ted was on the roof.

"Oh, there you are," said Pat.

"We've been looking all over for you. Whatever are you doing up there?"

"I'm mending this roof," said Ted,

"while the sun shines."

"Can you come down and sign for your

parcel?" said Pat.

"It's a bit tricky," said Ted.

"It really is a bit tricky, getting down

just now."

"Don't worry," said Pat.

"I'll come up."

Pat went up the ladder.

Jess wanted to see what was on Ted's
roof.
He followed Pat up the ladder.
On to the roof went Jess.

Over the roof and round the chimney
pots, after the birds.
"Hi, Jess, come back!" called Pat,
but Jess was not listening.

Ted signed Pat's book.

Pat went back down the ladder.

"I'm glad to be down again," said Pat.

"Now where is that cat of mine?

Come on, Jess! It's time to go. Jess! Jess!

Come on, you bad cat!"

Then he heard Ted call out,

"Look out, Jess!"

There was a thump.

Something rolled – rumble, rumble –

down the roof.

It banged into the gutter.

Pat looked up.

"Oh!"

Before he could move, something came

dripping and splashing on to him.

It was bright red...sticky...messy...

paint.

Jess had knocked over a pot of Ted's

paint.

You never saw such a mess!

It was all over Pat's hat.

There was some in his hair.

There was some on his nose.

Ted came down the ladder.

"Come on," said Ted.

"Quick, before it soaks in."

Pat and Ted ran into the kitchen.

Pat washed his hair and his nose.

Ted had a bottle under the sink.

"This is good stuff," he said.

He dabbed it on Pat's hat. It took a
deal of rubbing, and soaking, and
more dabs of the stuff from the bottle.

In the end, most of the paint came off.

"It's not too bad, now," said Ted.

"You'd better pop the hat in the washer
when you get home."

"Thanks," said Pat. "Now I wonder
where that cat's got to?"

Jess was at the top of the ladder,
mewing sadly.

"Poor Jess," said Ted. "He's stuck. He can go up ladders, but he cannot come down them. He's been stuck up there all this time."

Jess had red paint on his paws.

"He's been a pest," said Pat.

"A proper pest."

But Jess looked so sad,

Pat could not be cross with him.

He went up the ladder, and brought
Jess down, tucked inside his coat.

They had to rub Jess's paws with the
stuff in Ted's bottle to clean them...

and then they put him in the bath. Oh,

how he hated it!

He never, ever, went up a ladder again.

When Pat called at Granny Dryden's house, she brought a nice piece of fish out to the van for Jess on his own special plate.

Jess ate it up, and licked his lips, and purred.

He was much better after that.